Richard Scarry's
POSTMAN Pig
and His Busy Neighbors

A Random House PICTUREBACK® Book

Richard Scarry's

POST OFFICE

CANDY

TOWN HALL

Random House · New York

POSTMAN PiG
and His Busy Neighbors

RichardScarryBooks.com

Educators and librarians, for a variety of teaching tools, visit us at RHTeachersLibrarians.com

Library of Congress Control Number: 2013033654
ISBN 978-0-385-38419-3 (pbk.)

Printed in the United States of America
10 9 8 7 6 5 4 3 2 1

Random House Children's Books supports the First Amendment and celebrates the right to read.

Postman Pig delivers mail to all his busy neighbors in Busytown.
In the morning he picks up the letters and packages at the Busytown
post office. Then he starts his trip through town. He always begins at
the candy store.

Next, Postman Pig stops at the police station. Police Chief Charlie is in charge of keeping things peaceful in Busytown.

Sergeant Murphy chases after speeding cars.

Meter Maid Millie gives parking tickets to cars that are parked where they shouldn't be.

Snozzle, Sparky, and the other brave firemen put out any fires that start in Busytown.

Postman Pig has some mail for Dr. Lion. He gives it to Nurse Nelly.
She looks after all the sick people who are waiting to see the doctor.

Dr. Lion is examining a patient
in his office. He makes sure that
everyone in Busytown stays healthy.

Postman Pig delivers some magazines to Dr. Dentist's office. The dentist looks at Postman Pig's teeth.

"You have a nice smile," she says. "If you brush your teeth every day, it will stay that way."

Postman Pig next delivers mail to Druggist Dog. He also buys a new toothbrush to help him keep his nice smile.

GOOD GAS

TIRE SALE

GASOLINE

Postman Pig passes many more friendly neighbors on his way through town. Greasy George fills all the Busytown cars with gas.

Sadie, the tank-truck driver, delivers gasoline to Greasy George's station.

Wally, the window washer, washes all the windows in Busytown.

Sweeps, the street cleaner, keeps the streets neat and clean.

Don't walk under Wally's ladder, Postman Pig! It might bring bad luck.

SANITATION ENGINEERS

Rags and Bottles, the sanitation workers, haul the garbage away from all the Busytown homes.

Suddenly a strong wind begins to blow. But that does not stop Postman Pig.

He goes down a street where new houses are being built. Soon Postman Pig will be delivering mail to the people who move in.

Jason, the mason, is laying bricks for one of the new houses.

Sawdust, the carpenter, hammers at the frame of another new house.

Shingles, the roofer, nails shingles on a roof.

Switch, the electrician, puts in the electric wires.

Michelangelo, the painter, paints the outside of the house.

Faucet, the plumber, puts in water and sewage pipes.

Postman Pig has left a package for Libby, the librarian. She sees that the Busytown library has plenty of books for her busy neighbors to read.

Brownie, the taxi driver, takes people wherever they want to go in Busytown.

Many busy neighbors work in office buildings. Sally, the switchboard operator, makes sure that their telephone calls go through.

Carol, the secretary, manages the office for her boss.

Justice, the lawyer, helps people when they have problems with the laws of Busytown.

BUSYTOWN OFFICES

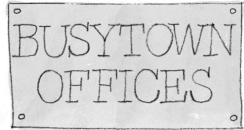

Postman Pig delivers mail to all these busy workers. He is glad because he likes to ride up and down in the elevator.

Postman Pig always stops off at the photo shop. He delivers film to be made into pictures. Today he also picks up some photos he has taken of his family.

Suddenly, rain starts pouring down. But it does NOT stop Postman Pig. And it does not stop Patience, the bus driver, from driving the Busytown children to school.

PHOTO SHOP   FILM

CHEESE SHOP   B

SCHOOL BUS

There is Sergeant Murphy again.
He is chasing a banana thief!

Postman Pig wonders what Busytown would
do without Miss Honey, the schoolteacher.
She is at the school from Monday to Friday,
teaching the Busytown children.

Now Postman Pig delivers a letter to the clothing store. While he is there, he buys a pretty dress for his little girl.

Snip-Snip, the barber, is the best barber ever. He keeps all the heads in Busytown looking neat and trim.

Postman Pig has to stop and get some money from the bank. The bank teller gives people their money when they need it to buy things. Busytown Bank is a good, safe place for all the busy neighbors to keep their money.

At the Busytown supermarket
Harry, the butcher, cuts up meat
for his customers.

Grocer Cat sells them fresh
fruit and vegetables.

Able Baker Charlie makes the most delicious cakes and breads anywhere.

Postman Pig buys a cake to take home with him. Can you guess why?

chef

waitress

waiter

MAIL

HOT DOGS

At last it is time for lunch. There are many different places to eat. Some neighbors eat delicious meals cooked by the chef at the Fried Egg Restaurant. Others like to eat at Cook Quick's Blue Train Special. But Postman Pig always eats a hot dog for lunch. Then he gets an ice cream stick for dessert.

Because of all the cars and trucks that use the Busytown roads, the streets often need to be repaired. The Busytown road-repair workers are very good at fixing them.

HARDWARE

FLORIST

Bugdozer

Oh, dear! Postman Pig has tripped and fallen into a ditch on his way to buy a flower for Mrs. Pig. But that will not stop him for long.

Farther down the street, Pat, the telephone woman, is fixing a broken telephone line.

Ole, the oilman, is filling a tank with oil so that the furnace will keep Mrs. Rabbit's house warm.

Poor Postman Pig! He has to wade
through a big puddle. Pipe, the handyman,
is trying to fix a leaky pipe. He usually
comes right away when anyone in
Busytown has a leak in the house.

Mr. Blessing, the clergyman, gets mail too. On holy days Busytown people come to worship with him.

Greenthumb, the gardener, keeps the public gardens neat and beautiful.

editor

linotype operator

press workers

THE DAILY SUN

NEWS

The Busytown newspaper tells everyone the latest news about what is happening in Busytown.

Some people buy their newspapers from the lady at the newsstand.

Other busy neighbors get their papers at home from a delivery boy or girl.

It is a long walk to Farmer Haystack's farm, but Postman Pig has a letter to deliver to him. Mrs. Haystack makes wonderful homemade jams and jellies to sell at her roadside stand. Postman Pig buys some jam and two dozen eggs.

Milton, the milkman, delivers milk all over Busytown. Someone is crying for her bottle right now.

At last Postman Pig arrives home after another hard day's work. He has delivered all the mail except one small package. That last package is for— POSTMAN PIG himself! What can it be?

Postman Pig opens the package and finds a GOLD WATCH! And on the watch are the words: "Because neither rain nor wind nor muddy ditches have kept you from delivering our daily mail, we—your Busytown neighbors—want to thank you and wish you a happy birthday!"

Postman Pig's family and their guest, Lowly Worm, all sit down to eat the birthday cake from Able Baker Charlie. Happy birthday, busy neighbor!